Food Fight Fiesta
A TALE ABOUT LA TOMATINA

TRACEY KYLE • Illustrated by: ANA GOMEZ

Sky Pony Press
New York

Grab a tomato . . .

get ready . . .

now

The world's largest food fight is starting right here in the town of Buñol, where we come once a year.

I put on my goggles and look for the truck
that hauls the tomatoes.

¡Caramba!
It's stuck!

We climb up the wheels and fall in a heap of squishy tomatoes and sink in knee-deep.

"Tomate, tomate,"

we hear the crowd sing.

We're ready to squash
the tomatoes and fling!
The truck moves in closer.
¡Olé! Here we go!

WHOOSH!

Tomatoes are filling the air.

They run down
my ankles and
squish in my toes.

Tomatoes are soaring and filling all spaces,
soaking our arms and our legs and our faces.

I slip and I slide in a river of red,
as a storm of tomatoes rains down on my head.

The crowd is soon covered in bright, crimson juice.

¡Caramba!
Tomatoes are still on the loose!

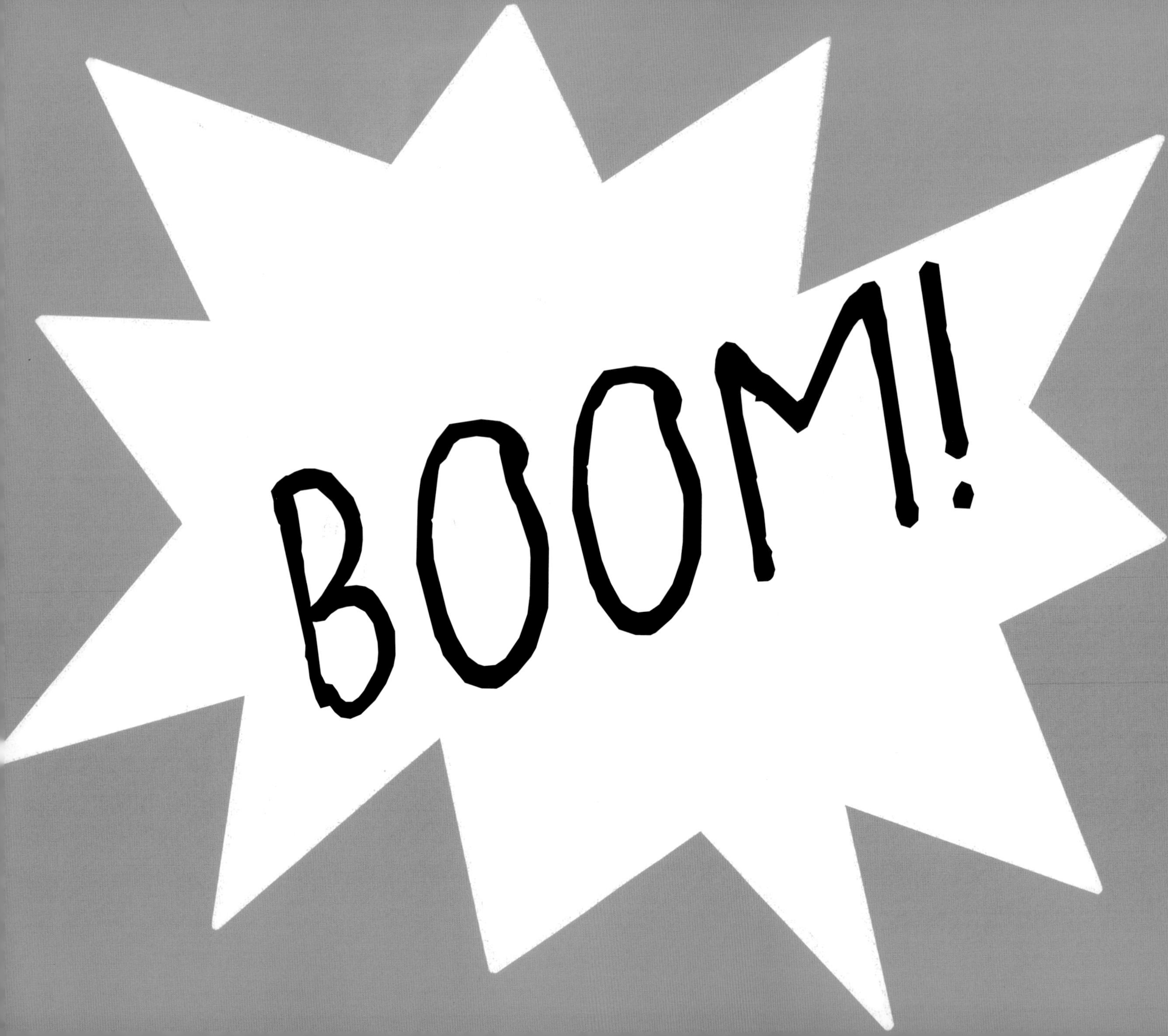
BOOM!

There's the signal to finish the fun.
The cannon has fired.

The festival's done.

It's time to stop throwing.
Let's all settle down.

The firemen show up to tidy the town.

We head to the river to rinse off the mess,
the pulp and the goo a sure sign of success.

The town of Buñol settles down for the night,
already dreaming of next year's food fight.

"*Tomate, tomate,*" I chant in my sleep,
cuddling a tomato I managed to keep.

AUTHOR'S NOTE

Are you ready to go to *La Tomatina*? Be prepared for a week full of activities because the big food fight isn't the only thing to look forward to. There are parades, musicians, fireworks, and a cooking contest for the tasty saffron-based rice and seafood dish of the region, paella.

Buñol, a small, quiet town in the province of Valencia, Spain, manages to welcome over 20,000 visitors the last Wednesday in August.

The annual fiesta began around 1945 and has grown in popularity as more and more people have heard about it thanks to the Internet. No one is sure how *La Tomatina* first came about, but today, participants honor the two patron saints of the town.

Because the *Tomatina* is so popular, you'll need to buy a ticket. Every hotel in town is full, and the plazas, parks, and streets are teeming with visitors from around the world.

Buildings are covered in plastic so they don't get stained during the food fight!

There are some rules: you must crush the tomatoes before you throw them; you can't rip or grab clothing; and you have to wear goggles to protect your eyes from the acid in the tomatoes.

¿Estás listo? Are you ready?

¡Diviértete! Have fun!

GLOSSARY

España • Eh-SPAHN-yah • Spain

Buñol • Boon-YOHL •
A small town in the region of Valencia, Spain. Buñol has a
   population of around 9,000, but more than 20,000 show
   up for *La Tomatina*!

¡Caramba! • Kah-RAHM-bah! • Wow! Good Grief!

¡Olé • Oh-LAY! • Hooray!

(el) tomate • Ehl-toh-MAH-tay • Tomato

BIBLIOGRAPHY

1. Gelling, Natasha. Photos from La Tomatina, the World's
   Biggest Food Fight. http://www.smithsonianmag.com.
   August 27, 2014.

2. Ibanez, Alberto. La Tomatina. Abriendo paso: Lectura.
   Authors: Jose M. Diaz, Stephen J. Collins, Maria F. Nadel.
   Upper Saddle River: Prentice Hall / Pearson Education;
   2nd ed. (2007) pp. 336 – 340.

3. La Tomatina Festival. Retrieved July 6, 2015 from http://www.
   latomatinatours.com.

WEBSITES
for kids on <<La Tomatina>> and Spain

1. www.kidzworld.com/article/1442-la-tomatina-festival
2. www.latomatina.info
3. www.donquijote.org/culture/spain/society/holidays/la-tomatina
4. www.dogonews.com/2010/8/26/la-tomatina-worlds-biggest-
   food-fight
5. kids.nationalgeographic.com/explore/countries/spain/
   #spain-cliffs.jpg

Para mis estudiantes
—Tracey Kyle

To Sergio
—Ana Gomez

Sky Pony Press books may be purchased at special discounts for sales promotion, corporate gifts, fund-raising, or educational purposes. Special editions can also be created to specifications. For details, contact the Special Sales Department, Sky Pony Press, 307 West 36th Street, 11th Floor, New York, NY 10018 or info@skyhorsepublishing.com.

Sky Pony® is a registered trademark of Skyhorse Publishing, Inc.®, a Delaware corporation.

Visit our website at www.skyponypress.com.

10 9 8 7 6 5 4 3 2 1

Manufactured in China, March 2018
This product conforms to CPSIA 2008

Library of Congress Cataloging-in-Publication Data
Names: Kyle, Tracey, author. | Gomez, Ana, 1977- illustrator.
Title: Food fight fiesta! : a tale of La Tomatina / Tracey Kyle ; Illustrated by Ana Gomez.
Description: New York : Sky Pony Press, [2018] | Summary: Illustrations and rhyming text depict the fiesta of La Tomatina, during which the small town of Bunol, Spain, becomes the site of a massive, tomato-throwing food fight. Includes facts about the festival and glossary of Spanish words. | Includes bibliographical references. |
Identifiers: LCCN 2017054924 (print) | LCCN 2018001525 (ebook) | ISBN 9781510732162 (eb) | ISBN 9781510732155 (print : alk. paper) | ISBN 9781510732162 (ebook)
Subjects: | CYAC: Stories in rhyme. | Festivals--Fiction. | Tomatoes--Fiction. | Bu?nol (Spain)--Fiction. | Spain--Fiction.
Classification: LCC PZ8.3.K984 (ebook) | LCC PZ8.3.K984 Fo 2018 (print) | DDC [E]--dc23
LC record available at https://lccn.loc.gov/2017054924

Cover illustration by Ana Gomez
Cover design by Kate Gartner